GREAT FAIRY TALE CLASSICS

THE THREE LITTLE PIGS
page 10

THE CRAB AND THE HERON
page 16

THE WOLF AND THE SEVEN KIDS
page 18

THE COUNTRY MOUSE AND THE TOWN MOUSE
page 24

THE UGLY DUCKLING
page 28

THE STORY OF THUMBELINA
page 34

THE ADVENTURES OF TOM THUMB
page 40

GOLDILOCKS AND THE THREE BEARS
page 44

THE HARE AND THE PORCUPINE
page 50

THE HARE AND THE ELEPHANT
page 54

ILLUSTRATED BY TONY WOLF
TEXT BY PETER HOLEINONE

© DAMI EDITORE, ITALY

Published by Tormont Publications Inc.
338 Saint Antoine St. E.
Montreal, Quebec
CANADA H2Y IA3

Printed in Italy

Printed by Officine Grafiche De Agostini S.p.A.
Bound by Legatoria del Verbano S.p.A.

The story of

THE THREE LITTLE PIGS

and other tales

Once upon a time . . .

. . . there was a very naughty wolf who wanted to eat three little pigs but the cleverest of the little pigs was more cunning than the wolf and this is their story . . .

THE THREE LITTLE PIGS

Once upon a time . . . there were three little pigs, who left their mummy and daddy to see the world.

All summer long, they roamed through the woods and over the plains, playing games and having fun. None were happier than the three little pigs, and they easily made friends with everyone. Wherever they went, they were given a warm welcome, but as summer drew to a close, they realised that folk were drifting back to their usual jobs, and preparing for winter. Autumn came and it began to rain. The three little pigs started to feel they needed a real home. Sadly they knew that the fun was over now and they must set to work like the others, or they'd be left in the cold and rain, with no roof over their heads. They talked about what to do, but each decided for himself. The laziest little pig said he'd build a straw hut.

"It will only take a day," he said. The others disagreed.

"It's too fragile," they said disapprovingly, but he refused to listen. Not quite so lazy, the second little pig went in search of planks of seasoned wood.

"Clunk! Clunk! Clunk!" It took him two days to nail them together. But the third little pig did not like the wooden house.

"That's not the way to build a house!" he said. "It takes time, patience and hard work to build a house that is strong enough to stand up to wind, rain, and snow, and most of all, protect us from the wolf!"

The days went by, and the wisest little pig's house took shape, brick by brick. From time to time, his brothers visited him, saying with a chuckle:

"Why are you working so hard? Why don't you come and play?" But the stubborn bricklayer pig just said "no".

"I shall finish my house first. It must be solid and sturdy. And *then* I'll come and play!" he said. "I shall not be foolish like you! For he who laughs last, laughs longest!"

It was the wisest little pig that found the tracks of a big wolf in the neighbourhood.

The little pigs rushed home in alarm. Along came the wolf, scowling fiercely at the laziest pig's straw hut.

"Come out!" ordered the wolf, his mouth watering. "I want to speak to you!"

"I'd rather stay where I am!" replied the little pig in a tiny voice.

"I'll make you come out!" growled the wolf angrily, and puffing out his chest, he took a very deep breath. Then he blew with all his might, right onto the house. And all the straw the silly pig had heaped against some thin poles, fell down in the great blast. Excited by his own cleverness, the wolf did not notice that the little pig had slithered out from underneath the heap of straw, and was dashing towards his brother's wooden house.

When he realised that the little pig was escaping, the wolf grew wild with rage.

"Come back!" he roared, trying to catch the pig as he ran into the wooden house. The other little pig greeted his brother, shaking like a leaf.

"I hope this house won't fall down! Let's lean against the door so he can't break in!"

Outside, the wolf could hear the little pigs' words. Starving as he was, at the idea of a two-course meal, he rained blows on the door.

"Open up! Open up! I only want to speak to you!" he lied. Inside, the two brothers wept in fear and did their best to hold the door fast against the blows. Then the furious wolf braced himself for a new effort: he drew in a really enormous breath, and went . . . WHOOOOO! The wooden house collapsed like a pack of cards.

Luckily, the wisest little pig had been watching the scene from the window of his own brick house, and he rapidly opened the door to his fleeing brothers. And not a moment too soon, for the wolf was already hammering furiously on the door. This time, the wolf had grave doubts. This house had a much more solid air

than the others. He blew once, he blew again and then for a third time. But all was in vain. For the house did not budge an inch. The three little pigs watched him and their fear began to fade. Quite exhausted by his efforts, the wolf decided to try one of his tricks. He scrambled up a nearby ladder, on to the roof to have a look at the chimney. However, the wisest little pig had seen this ploy, and he quickly said:

"Quick! Light the fire!" With his long legs thrust down the chimney, the wolf was not sure if he should slide down the black hole. It wouldn't be easy to get in, but the sound of the little pigs' voices below only made him feel hungrier.

"I'm dying of hunger! I'm going to try and get down." And he let himself drop. But his landing was rather hot, too hot! The wolf landed in the fire, stunned by his fall.

The flames licked his hairy coat and his tail became a flaring torch.

"Never again! Never again will I go down a chimney!" he squealed, as he tried to put out the flames in his tail. Then he ran away as fast as he could.

The three happy little pigs, dancing round and round the yard, began to sing:

"Tra-la-la! Tra-la-la! The wicked black wolf will never come back. . . !"

From that terrible day on, the wisest little pig's brothers set to work with a will. In less than no time, up went the two new brick houses. The wolf did return once to roam in the neighbourhood,

but when he caught sight of *three* chimneys, he remembered the terrible pain of a burnt tail, and he left for good.

Now safe and happy, the wisest little pig called to his brothers: "No more work! Come on, let's go and play!"

THE CRAB AND THE HERON

Once upon a time . . . an elderly heron made his home in a pond full of fish. He was stiff and slow in his old age, and he didn't find it easy to catch his lunch.

However, he decided to use his wits: he went to see a crab, said to be a great chatterbox, and in a mock frightened voice, told him the latest rumour.

"Certain birds, friends of mine, say that the lakeside fishermen will be coming here soon with their nets. They're going to take away all the fish. I'll have no meals left. Everything will be gone and the fish will end up in the frying pan!"

The crab quickly scuttled away to the banks of the pond and dived in to tell the fish the awful news. The frightened fish begged the crab for good advice, and he returned to the heron.

". . . they're all scared stiff and don't know which way to turn. While you yourself snap up a few now and again, it's against your interests if they go. So what shall we do?" The heron pretended to be lost in thought. Then he said: "I'll tell you what! I can carry them, a few at a time, to a pond hidden in the forest. They'll be

quite safe there. But will the fish trust me?"

Whether they were scared of the fishermen, or maybe the crab had a glib tongue, at any rate, the fish agreed to this strange offer. The heron began his trips between pond and forest. But the crab noticed that the heron made excuses for dallying on the way. What was more, the crab's keen eye noticed that the heron's tummy was now a good deal plumper. Days later, when all the fish had been rescued from the pond, the heron said to the crab: "Don't you want to be rescued too?" he asked.

"Certainly!" replied the crab.

"Bend over. I'll climb on to your neck. I'd hate to make your beak tired!"

When they were far from the pond, the crab saw that the ground was littered with fish bones. He clung tightly to the heron's neck with his strong pincers, and said: "I've no intention of coming to the same bad end as the fish! Now, just deposit me gently into the water. I'm not letting go of your neck till I feel safe!"

And from that day on, crabs and herons have always loathed each other and try to avoid meeting.

THE WOLF AND THE SEVEN KIDS

Once upon a time . . . a Mother Goat lived in a pretty little house with her seven kids. Mother often had to leave home to do the shopping, and on that fateful day, she had given her children the usual warnings, before setting off to market.

"You mustn't open the door to anyone. Don't forget, there's a wicked wolf lurking about here. It's black, with horrible paws and a nasty deep voice. If it knocks, keep the door tightly shut!"
Mother Goat's words were wise indeed, for as she was telling one of her neighbours about her fears, the wolf disguised as a peasant, was hiding close by, listening to every word.

"Good! Very good!" said the wolf to himself. "If the goat goes to market, I'll drop by her house and gobble the kids!" Then, trying

not to look too conspicuous, the wolf hurried along to the goat's house. There, he threw off his disguise. He then growled in a deep voice: "Open the door! Open the door! It's Mother! I've just come back from market! Open the door!" When the kids heard the deep voice, they remembered their mother's warning. From behind the barred door, they said to the wolf: "We know who you are! You're the wolf! Our mother has a sweet gentle voice, not a deep nasty one like yours! Go away! We'll never open the door to you!"

And though the wolf banged furiously on the door, the kids, though trembling with terror, refused to let him into the house, and so the door remained shut. Then the wolf had a brainwave. He dashed off to the baker's and got a big

cake dripping with honey. He hoped this would sweeten his
voice. And in fact, after eating it, his voice didn't sound quite so
deep. Over and over again, he practised imitating Mother Goat's
voice. You see, he'd heard it in the woods. When he felt certain
he could easily be mistaken for Mother Goat herself, he rushed
back to the house and the seven kids.

"Open the door! Open the door! It's Mother! I've just come
back from market! Open the door!" he called. This time, the kids
had doubts: the voice *did* rather sound like mother's, and they
were about to unlock the
door, when the black kid
suspiciously cried: "Mother,
let us see your foot!" Without
thinking, the wolf raised a
black hairy paw. And the kids
knew that the wolf had come
back.

"You're not our mother!
She doesn't have horrid
black paws!" cried the kids.
"Go away, you wicked wolf!"

And once more, in spite of
all his hard work, the wolf

found the door locked against him. The wolf ran down to the mill, and found a sack of flour. He thrust his paws into it until they were pure white.

"I'll trick them this time," he said. "Mmm! My mouth's watering already! I'm hungry! My tummy's empty and my trousers are falling off! I'll swallow these tender kids whole!" Again he knocked on the door.

"Open the door! Open the door! It's Mother! I've just come back from market! Open the door!" The voice seemed exactly like mother's, but the wary kids quickly called out: "Mother, let us see your foot!" The wily wolf lifted a snow white paw, and the kids, now reassured, threw

open the door. What a shock they received! An enormous set of jaws with sharp fangs growled fiercely. Cruel claws reached out for their prey. The kids scattered in terror. One dived under the table, while another crawled below the bed. Another kid hid in the cupboard and one tried to hide in the oven, though the stove was still hot. One kid crouched inside a barrel and one hid in the grandfather clock. There he huddled, holding his breath, as the wolf hunted down his brothers. One by one, the kids were pulled from their hiding places. All except for the kid in the clock. The wicked wolf's appetite did not pass until he had found them and swallowed each in a single gulp.

The only one to escape was the little black kid, for the wolf never imagined that there was room for a kid inside the very narrow grandfather clock. In the meantime, Mother Goat had really come back from market. When, from a distance, she noticed that the door was

ajar, she rushed home, her heart in her mouth. She had a sinking feeling: what she feared had really happened. The wicked wolf had gobbled up all her children. She dropped into a chair, sobbing bitterly, but as she cried, the door of the grandfather clock swung open and out ran the black kid.

"Mummy! Mummy!" wept the kid. "It was terrible! The wolf came, and I think he's eaten all my brothers!"

"My poor child!" sobbed Mother Goat. "You're the only one left! That evil brute has gobbled them all!"

Not long after, Mother Goat and her son left the house to take a stroll in the garden. Suddenly, she heard a low wheezing sound: someone was snoring heavily. It was the greedy wolf. His feast of kids had been too much for him and he was fast asleep, dead to the world. In a flash, Mother Goat had a brainwave. She said to her son: "Run and fetch me a needle and thread and a pair of scissors!" With these, she swiftly slit open the wolf's stomach. As she had hoped, the ravenous brute had swallowed every kid whole. There they were, all still alive inside his tummy. One by one, out they popped from the wolf's tummy.

"Hurry! Hurry! Not a sound! We must get away before he wakens up! Wait! Fetch me a heap of stones!" And so they filled the wolf's stomach with stones and stitched it up again. The wolf woke later with a raging thirst.

"What a heavy tummy I have!" he said. "I've eaten too much! All these kids!" But when he went down to the river to drink, his tummy full of stones tipped him over and he fell into the water. The weight took him straight to the bottom, and the goat and her kids shrieked with joy as he sank. The wicked wolf was dead and the kids trotted home happily with Mother.

THE COUNTRY MOUSE
AND THE TOWN MOUSE

Once upon a time . . . a town mouse, on a trip to the country, met a country mouse. They spent the day together and became friends. The country mouse took his new friend into the meadows and vegetable gardens, making him sample all the good things of the land. Never having seen the beauties of the countryside, the town mouse was thrilled, though the country mouse's plain food wasn't nearly as fine as his own usual meals. To thank his friend for the lovely outing, he invited the country mouse to visit him in the town. And when the country mouse saw the pantry at his friend's house, full of hams, cheese, oil, flour, honey, jam and stacks of other goodies, he stood speechless with surprise.

"I've never seen anything like it! Are all those wonderful things for eating?"

"Of course!" came the reply. "You're my guest, so tuck in!" They began

to feast, while the country mouse tried not to stuff himself. He wanted to taste *everything* before finding his tummy full.

"You're the luckiest mouse I've ever met!" said the country mouse to his town brother. The town mouse was listening with delight to his friend's praise, when suddenly, the sound of heavy footsteps interrupted their feast.

"Run for it!" whispered the town mouse to his friend. They were just in time: for within an inch of them stood the lady of the house's large foot! What a fright! Luckily, the lady went away and the two mice returned to enjoy their meal, so rudely interrupted.

"It's all right! Come on!" said the town mouse. "Don't worry. She's gone. Now for the honey! It's delicious! Have you ever tasted it?"

"Yes, once, a long time ago," the country mouse lied, trying to sound casual. But when he tasted it, he exclaimed: "Scrumptious! By

the King of Mice! I've never eaten anything so lovely in all my life!"

Suddenly there came the sound of footsteps, this time thumping heavily. The two mice fled. The man of the house had come to fetch some bottles, and when he saw the spilt honey, he groaned: "Those ghastly mice again! I thought I'd got rid of them. I'll send the cat!" And trembling with terror, the mice hid away. This time it was

not only the sudden visit that had given them a fright, it was the man's awful words. The mice were so scared, they held their breath, making no sound. Then, since all remained quiet, they began to feel braver, and picked up enough courage to leave their hidey-hole.

"We can come out now! There's nobody here!" the town mouse whispered.

Suddenly, the pantry door creaked, and the two luckless mice froze in fear. Out of the dim light

glowed a pair of horrid yellow eyes. A large cat was staring round the room in search of its prey. The country mouse and the town mouse tiptoed silently back to their hidey-hole. They wished their pounding hearts would stop beating, for fear of the cat hearing the noise they made. But, as luck would have it, the cat discovered a juicy sausage. Forgetting why his master had sent him into the pantry, he stopped to eat it. No longer hungry, after that, the cat decided that he might as well leave mouse-hunting for another day. Off he padded, to have forty winks elsewhere. Now, as soon as the country mouse realized that all danger was past, he did not lose a second. He hastily shook hands with his friend, saying: Thanks so much for everything! But I must rush off now! I can't stand all these shocks! I'd far rather sit down to a meal of a few acorns in peace, in the country, than face a great spread of delicious food, surrounded by dangers on all sides and with my heart in my mouth!"

THE UGLY DUCKLING

Once upon a time . . . down on an old farm, lived a duck family, and Mother Duck had been sitting on a clutch of new eggs. One nice morning, the eggs hatched and out popped six chirpy ducklings. But one egg was bigger than the rest, and it didn't hatch. Mother Duck couldn't recall laying that seventh egg. How did it get there? TOCK! TOCK! The little prisoner was pecking inside his shell.

"Did I count the eggs wrongly?" Mother Duck wondered. But before she had time to think about it, the last egg finally hatched. A strange looking duckling with grey feathers that should have been yellow gazed at a worried mother. The ducklings grew quickly, but Mother Duck had a secret worry.

"I can't understand how this ugly duckling can be one of mine!" she said to herself, shaking her head as she looked at her lastborn. Well, the grey duckling certainly wasn't pretty, and since he ate far more than his brothers, he was outgrowing them. As the days went by, the poor ugly duckling became more and more unhappy. His brothers didn't want to play with him, he was so clumsy, and all the farmyard folks simply laughed at him. He felt sad and lonely, while Mother Duck did her best to console him.

"Poor little ugly duckling!" she would say. "Why are you so different from the others?" And the ugly duckling felt worse than ever. He secretly wept at night. He felt nobody wanted him.

"Nobody loves me, they all tease me! Why am I different from my brothers?"

Then one day, at sunrise, he ran away from the farmyard. He stopped at a pond and began to

question all the other birds: "Do you know of any ducklings with grey feathers like mine?" But everyone shook their heads in scorn.

"We don't know anyone as ugly as you." The ugly duckling did not lose heart, however, and kept on making enquiries. He went

to another pond, where a pair of large geese gave him the same answer to his question. What's more, they warned him: "Don't stay here! Go away! It's dangerous. There are men with guns around here!" The duckling was sorry he had ever left the farmyard.

Then one day, his travels took him near an old countrywoman's cottage. Thinking he was a stray goose, she caught him.

"I'll put this in a hutch. I hope it's a female and lays plenty of eggs!" said the old woman, whose eyesight was poor. But the ugly duckling laid not a single egg. The hen kept frightening him:

"Just wait! If you don't lay eggs, the old woman will wring your neck and pop you into the pot!" And the cat chipped in: "Hee! Hee! I hope the woman cooks you soon, then I can gnaw at your bones!" The poor ugly duckling was so scared that he lost his appetite, though the old woman kept stuffing him with food and grumbling: "If you won't lay eggs, at least hurry up and get plump!"

"Oh, dear me!" moaned the now terrified duckling. "I'll die of fright first! And I did so hope someone would love me!"

Then one night, finding the hutch door ajar, he escaped. Once again he was all alone. He fled as far away as he could, and at dawn, he found himself in a thick bed of reeds. "If nobody wants me, I'll hide here forever." There was plenty of food, and the duckling began to feel a little happier, though he was lonely. One day at sunrise, he saw a flight of beautiful birds wing overhead. White, with long slender necks, yellow beaks and large wings, they were migrating south.

"If only I could look like them, just for a day!" said the duckling, admiringly. Winter came and the water in the reed bed froze. The poor duckling left home to seek food in the snow. He dropped exhausted to the ground, but a farmer found him and put him in his big jacket pocket.

"I'll take him home to my children. They'll look after him. Poor thing, he's frozen!" The duckling was showered with kindly care at the farmer's house. In this way, the ugly duckling was able to survive the bitterly cold winter.

However, by springtime, he had grown so big that the farmer decided: "I'll set him free by the pond!" That was when the duckling saw himself mirrored in the water.

"Goodness! How I've changed! I hardly recognise myself!" The flight of swans winged north again and glided on to the pond. When the duckling saw them, he realised he was one of their kind, and soon made friends.

"We're swans like you!" they said, warmly. "Where have you been hiding?"

"It's a long story," replied the young swan, still astounded. Now, he swam majestically with his fellow swans. One day, he heard children on the river bank exclaim: "Look at that young swan! He's the finest of them all!"

And he almost burst with happiness.

THE STORY OF THUMBELINA

Once upon a time . . . there lived a
woman who had no children. She
dreamed of having a little girl, but time went by,
and her dream never came true.

She then went to visit a witch, who gave her a
magic grain of barley. She planted it in a flower
pot. And the very next day, the grain had turned
into a lovely flower, rather like a tulip. The
woman softly kissed its half-shut petals. And as though by
magic, the flower opened in full blossom. Inside sat a tiny girl,
no bigger than a thumb. The woman called her Thumbelina.
For a bed she had a walnut shell, violet petals for her mattress
and a rose petal blanket. In the daytime, she played in a tulip
petal boat, floating on a plate of water. Using two horse hairs as
oars, Thumbelina sailed around her little lake, singing and
singing in a gentle sweet voice.

Then one night, as she lay fast asleep in her walnut shell, a
large frog hopped through a hole in the window pane. As she
gazed down at Thumbelina, she said to herself: "How pretty she
is! She'd make the perfect bride for my own dear son!"

She picked up Thumbelina, walnut shell and all, and hopped into the garden. Nobody saw her go. Back at the pond, her fat ugly son, who always did as mother told him, was pleased with her choice. But mother frog was afraid that her pretty prisoner might run away. So she carried Thumbelina out to a water lily leaf in the middle of the pond.

"She can never escape us now," said the frog to her son.

"And we have plenty of time to prepare a new home for you and your bride." Thumbelina was left all alone. She felt so desperate. She knew she would never be able to escape the fate that awaited her with the two horrid fat frogs. All she could do was cry her eyes out. However, one or two minnows who had been enjoying the shade below the water lily leaf, had overheard the two frogs talking, and the little girl's bitter sobs. They decided to do

something about it. So they nibbled away at the lily stem till it broke and drifted away in the weak current. A dancing butterfly had an idea: "Throw me the end of your belt! I'll help you to move a little faster!" Thumbelina gratefully did so, and the leaf soon floated away from the frog pond.

But other dangers lay ahead. A.

large beetle snatched Thumbelina with his strong feet and took her away to his home at the top of a leafy tree.

"Isn't she pretty?" he said to his friends. But they pointed out that she was far too different. So the beetle took her down the tree and set her free.

It was summertime, and Thumbelina wandered all by herself amongst the flowers and through the long grass. She had pollen for her meals and drank the dew. Then the rainy season came, bringing nasty weather. The poor child found it hard to find food and shelter. When winter set in, she suffered from the cold and felt terrible pangs of hunger.

One day, as Thumbelina roamed helplessly over the bare meadows, she met a large spider who promised to help her. He took her to a hollow tree and guarded the door with a stout web. Then he brought her some dried chestnuts and called his friends to come and admire her beauty. But just like the beetles, all the other spiders persuaded Thumbelina's rescuer to let her go. Crying her heart out, and quite certain that nobody wanted her because she was ugly, Thumbelina left the spider's house.

As she wandered, shivering with the cold, suddenly she came across a solid little cottage, made of twigs and dead leaves. Hopefully, she knocked on the door. It was opened by a field mouse.

"What are you doing outside in this weather?" he asked. "Come in and warm youself." Comfortable and cosy, the field mouse's home was stocked with food. For her keep, Thumbelina did the housework and told the mouse stories. One day, the field mouse said a friend was coming to visit them.

"He's a very rich mole, and has a lovely house. He wears a splendid black fur coat, but he's dreadfully shortsighted. He needs company and he'd like to marry you!" Thumbelina did not relish the idea. However, when the mole came, she sang sweetly to him and he fell head over heels in love. The mole invited Thumbelina and the field mouse to visit him, but . . . to their surprise and horror, they came upon a swallow in the tunnel. It looked dead. Mole nudged it with his foot, saying: "That'll teach her! She should have come underground instead of darting about the sky all summer!" Thumbelina was so shocked by such cruel words that later, she crept back unseen to the tunnel.

And every day, the little girl went to nurse the swallow and tenderly give it food.

In the meantime, the swallow told Thumbelina its tale. Jagged by a thorn, it had been unable to follow its companions to a warmer climate.

"It's kind of you to nurse me," it told Thumbelina. But, in spring, the swallow flew away, after offering to take the little girl with it. All summer, Thumbelina did her best to avoid marrying the mole. The little girl thought fearfully of how she'd have to live underground forever. On the eve of her wedding, she asked to spend a day in the open air. As she gently fingered a flower, she heard a familiar song: "Winter's on its way and I'll be off to warmer lands. Come with me!" Thumbelina quickly clung to her swallow friend, and the bird soared into the sky. They flew over plains and hills till they reached a country of flowers. The swallow gently laid Thumbelina in a blossom. There she met a tiny, white-winged fairy: the King of the Flower Fairies. Instantly, he asked her to marry him. Thumbelina eagerly said "yes", and sprouting tiny white wings, she became the Flower Queen!

THE ADVENTURES OF
TOM THUMB

Once upon a time . . . there lived a giant who had quarrelled with a very greedy wizard over sharing a treasure. After the quarrel, the giant said menacingly to the wizard:

"I could crush you under my thumb if I wanted to! Now, get out of my sight!" The wizard hurried away, but from a safe distance, he hurled his terrible revenge.

"Abracadabra! Here I cast this spell! May the son, your wife will shortly give you, never grow any taller than my own thumb!"

After Tom Thumb was born, his parents were at their wits' end. They could never find him, for they could barely *see* him. They had to speak in whispers for fear of deafening the little boy. Tom Thumb preferred playing with the little garden creatures, to the company of parents so different from himself. He rode piggyback on the snail and danced with the ladybirds. Tiny as he was, he had great fun in the world of little things.

But one unlucky day, he went to visit a froggy friend. No sooner had he scrambled onto a leaf than a large pike swallowed him up. But the pike too was fated to come to a very bad end. A

little later, he took the bait cast by one of the King's fishermen, and before long, found himself under the cook's knife in the royal kitchens. And great was everyone's surprise when, out of the fish's stomach, stepped Tom Thumb, quite alive and little the worse for his adventure.

"What am I to do with this tiny lad?" said the cook to himself. Then he had a brainwave. "He can be a royal pageboy! He's so tiny, I can pop him into the cake I'm making. When he marches across the bridge, sounding the trumpet, everyone will gasp in wonder!" Never had such a marvel been seen at Court. The guests clapped excitedly at the cook's skill and the King himself clapped loudest of all. The King rewarded the clever cook with a bag of gold. Tom Thumb was even luckier. The cook made him a pageboy, and a pageboy he remained, enjoying all the honours of his post.

He had a white mouse for a mount, a gold pin for a sword and he was allowed to eat the King's food. In exchange, he marched up and down the table at banquets. He picked his way amongst the plates and glasses, amusing the guests with his trumpet.

What Tom Thumb didn't know was that he had made an enemy. The cat which, until Tom's arrival, had been the King's pet, was now forgotten. And, vowing to have its revenge on the newcomer, it ambushed Tom in the garden. When Tom saw the cat, he did not run away, as the creature had intended. He whipped out his gold pin and cried to his white mouse mount:

"Charge! Charge!" Jabbed by the tiny sword, the cat turned tail and fled. Since brute force was

not the way to revenge, the cat decided to use guile. Casually pretending to bump into the King as he walked down the staircase, the cat softly miaowed:

"Sire! Be on your guard! A plot is being hatched against your life!" And then he told a dreadful lie. "Tom Thumb is planning to lace your food with hemlock. I saw him picking the leaves in the garden the other day. I heard him say these very words!"

Now, the King had once been kept in bed with very bad tummy pains, after eating too many cherries and he feared the thought of being poisoned, so he sent for Tom

Thumb. The cat provided proof of his words by pulling a hemlock leaf from under the white mouse's saddle cloth, where he had hidden it himself.

Tom Thumb was so amazed, he was at a loss for words to deny what the cat had said. The King, without further ado, had him thrown into prison. And since he was so tiny, they locked him up in a pendulum clock. The hours passed and the days too. Tom's only pastime was swinging back and forth, clinging to the pendulum, until the night when he attracted the attention of a big night moth, fluttering round the room.

"Let me out!" cried Tom Thumb, tapping on the glass. As it so happens, the moth had only just been set free after being a prisoner in a large box, in which she had taken a nap. So she took pity on Tom Thumb and released him.

"I'll take you to the Butterfly Kingdom, where everyone's tiny like yourself. They'll take care of you there!" And that is what happened. To this day, if you visit the Butterfly Kingdom, you can ask to see the butterfly monument that Tom Thumb built after this amazing adventure.

GOLDILOCKS
AND THE
THREE BEARS

Once upon a time . . . in a large forest, close to a village, stood the cottage where the Teddy Bear family lived. They were not really proper Teddy Bears, for Father Bear was very big, Mother Bear was middling in size, and only Baby Bear could be described as a *Teddy* Bear.

Each bear had its own size of bed. Father Bear's was large and nice and comfy. Mother Bear's bed was middling in size, while Baby Bear had a fine little cherrywood bed that Father Bear had ordered from a couple of beaver friends.

Beside the fireplace, around which the family sat in the evenings, stood a large carved chair for the head of the house, a delightful blue velvet armchair for Mother Bear, and a very little chair for Baby Bear.

Neatly laid out on the kitchen table stood three china bowls. A large one for Father Bear, a smaller one for Mother Bear, and a little bowl for Baby Bear.

The neighbours were all very respectful to Father Bear and people raised their hats when he went by. Father Bear liked that and he always politely replied to their greetings. Mother Bear had lots of friends. She visited them in the afternoons to exchange good advice and recipes for jam and bottled fruit. Baby Bear, however, had hardly any friends. This was partly because he was rather a bully and liked to win games and arguments. He was a pest too and always getting into mischief. Not far away, lived a fair-haired little girl who had a similar nature to Baby Bear, only she was haughty and stuck-up as well, and though Baby Bear often asked her to come and play at his house, she always said no.

One day, Mother Bear made a nice pudding. It was a new recipe, with blueberries and other crushed berries. Her friends told her it was delicious. When it was ready, she said to the family:

"It has to be left to cool now, otherwise it won't taste nice. That will take at least an hour. Why don't we go and visit the Beavers' new baby? Mummy Beaver will be pleased to see us." Father Bear and Baby Bear would much rather have tucked into the pudding, warm or not, but they liked the thought of visiting the new baby.

"We must wear our best clothes, even for such a short visit. Everyone at the Beavers' will be very busy now, and we must not stay too long!" And so they set off along the pathway towards the river bank. A short time later, the stuck-up little girl, whose name was Goldilocks, passed by the Bears' house as she picked flowers.

"Oh, what an ugly house the Bears have!" said Goldilocks to herself as she went down the hill. "I'm going to peep inside! It won't be beautiful like my house, but I'm dying to see where Baby Bear lives." Knock! Knock! The little girl tapped on the door. Knock! Knock! Not a sound . . .

"Surely someone will hear me knocking," Goldilocks said to herself, impatiently. "Anyone at home?" she called, peering round the door. Then she went into the empty house and started to explore the kitchen.

"A pudding!" she cried, dipping a finger into the pudding Mother Bear had left to cool. "Quite nice! Quite nice!" she murmured, spooning it from Baby Bear's bowl. In a twinkling, the bowl lay empty on a messy table. With a full tummy, Goldilocks went on exploring.

"Now then, this must be Father Bear's chair, this will be Mother Bear's, and this one . . . must belong to my friend, Baby Bear. I'll just sit on it a while!" With these words, Goldilocks sat herself down onto the little chair which, quite unused to such a sudden weight, promptly broke a leg. Goldilocks crashed to the floor, but not in the least dismayed by the damage she had done, she went upstairs.

There was no mistaking which was Baby Bear's bed.

"Mm! Quite comfy!" she said, bouncing on it. "Not as nice as mine, but nearly!" Then she yawned. "I think I'll lie down, only for a minute . . . just to try the bed." And in next to no time, Goldilocks lay fast asleep in Baby Bear's bed. In the meantime, the Bears were on their way home.

"Wasn't the new Beaver baby ever so small?" said Baby Bear to his mother. "Was I as tiny as that when I was born?"

"Not quite, but almost," came the reply, with a fond caress. From a distance, Father Bear noticed the door was ajar.

"Hurry!" he cried. "Someone is in our house . . ." Was Father Bear hungry or did a thought strike him? Anyway, he dashed into the kitchen. "I knew it! Somebody has gobbled up the pudding . . ."

"Someone has been jumping up and down on my armchair!" complained Mother Bear.

". . . and somebody's broken my chair!" wailed Baby Bear.

Where could the culprit be? They all ran upstairs and tiptoed in amazement over to Baby Bear's bed. In it lay Goldilocks, sound asleep. Baby Bear prodded her toe . . .

"Who's that? Where am I?" shrieked the little girl, waking with a start. Taking fright at the scowling faces bending over her, she clutched the bedclothes up to her chin. Then she jumped out of bed and fled down the stairs.

"Get away! Away from that house!" she told herself as she ran, forgetful of all the trouble she had so unkindly caused. But Baby Bear called from the door, waving his arm:

"Don't run away! Come back! I forgive you . . . come and play with me!"

And this is how it all ended. From that day onwards, haughty rude Goldilocks became a pleasant little girl. She made friends with Baby Bear and often went to his house. She invited him to her house too, and they remained good friends, always.

THE HARE AND THE PORCUPINE

Once upon a time . . . an old porcupine lived in a large wood with his twin sons. Apples were their favourite dish, but the youngsters sometimes raided a neighbouring vegetable plot for the turnips Dad loved to munch. One day, one of the young porcupines set off as usual to fetch the turnips. Like all porcupines, he was a slow walker, and he had just reached a large cabbage, when from behind the leaves, out popped a hare.

"So you have arrived at last!" said the hare. "I've been watching you for half an hour. Do you always dawdle? I hope you're quicker at eating, or it will take you a year to finish the turnips!" Instead of going into a huff at being teased, the porcupine decided to get his own back

by being very crafty.

Slow on his feet but a quick thinker, he rapidly hit on a plan. So the hare sneered at the slow porcupine, did he? Well, the hare's own turn of speed would be his downfall!

"I can run faster than you if I try," said the porcupine. "Ha! Ha!" the hare shrieked with laughter, raising a large paw. "You can't compete with this! My grandad was the speediest hare of his day. He even won a gold penny. He used to be my coach. And you tell me you can run faster than me? Well, I bet my grandad's gold penny that I can win without even trying!"

The porcupine paid little heed to the hare's boastful words and quietly accepted the challenge. "I'll meet you tomorrow down at the ploughed field. We'll race in parallel furrows. And see who wins!"

The hare went away laughing.

"Better stay here all night! You'll never get home and back in time for the race!" he told the porcupine. The porcupine, however, had a bright idea. When he arrived home, he told his twin brother what had happened. Just before dawn next day, he gave him his instructions, and off they set for the

field. Hare appeared, rudely remarking: "I'll take off my jacket so I can run faster!"

Ready! Steady! Go! And in a flash, the hare streaked to the other end of the field. There, waiting for him was a porcupine, which teasingly said:

"Rather late, aren't you? I've been here for ages!" Gasping and so breathless his throat was dry, the hare whispered: "Let's try again!"

"All right," agreed the porcupine, "we'll run the race again." Never in all his life had the hare run so fast. Not even with the hounds snapping at his heels. But every time he reached the other end of the ploughed field, what did he find but the porcupine, who laughingly exclaimed: "What? Late again? I keep on getting here first!" Racing up and down the field, the hare sped, trying to beat the porcupine. His legs grew terribly tired and he began to sag. And every time he came to the end of the field, there stood a porcupine calling himself the winner.

"Perhaps I ought to mention, friend hare, that my grandad was the fastest porcupine of his day. He didn't win a gold

penny, but he won apples, and after the race, he ate them. But I don't want apples. I'd rather have the nice gold penny you promised me!" said one of the porcupine twins.

The hare slid to the ground, dead tired. His head was spinning and his legs felt like rubber.

"This race is the end of me! I shall die here in this field, where I really believed I was a sprinter! The shame of it! What a disgrace!" The hare staggered home, hot and sticky, to fetch the gold penny that he had never for a moment ever imagined he would lose. His eyes brimming with tears, he handed it over to the porcupines.

"Thank goodness my grandad isn't alive to see this!" he said. "Whatever would he say? After all his coaching, here I am, beaten by a porcupine!"

That evening, a party was held at the porcupines' house. The twins danced triumphantly in turn, waving aloft the gold penny. Father Porcupine brought out his old accordion for the special occasion, and the fun went on all night. As luck would have it, the hare never did find out the secret of how the race had been rigged. Which was just as well! . . .

THE HARE
AND THE ELEPHANT

Once upon a time . . . in the Indian jungle, lived a young elephant whose playmate was a very large hare. In spite of the difference in size, they were great friends and had fun playing strange guessing games. One day, the hare said to his chum:

"Which of us is bigger: you or me?" At that silly question, the little elephant nearly choked on his banana.

"You must be joking!" he exclaimed. "Why, even on tiptoe, you're not as high as my knee!" But the hare went on:

"That's what *you* think! Since *I* say that I'm bigger than you, we need a judge. Don't you agree?"

"Oh, yes," said the elephant in surprise.

"Well, let's go along to the village and see what the Humans have to say. They're the cleverest of all the animals, and the best judges!" As they reached the village, they met some of the villagers.

"Look at that young elephant! Isn't he small?" folk remarked as the unusual couple strolled by.

"Yes, he is indeed! But he'll soon grow up," said

others. Then somebody noticed the hare.

"What a huge hare!" they all cried. Now, the hare tried to keep in front of the elephant and puffed out his chest. As he passed, all the villagers exclaimed:

"Look at his paws! And those ears! That's the biggest hare we've ever seen!" When he heard this, the hare turned to his friend, saying,

"We can go home now! That's settled! I'm huge and you're tiny!" The elephant tossed his heavy head. At a loss for words, he knew the hare had won by low cunning. But back on the jungle path, he lifted his foot and said to the hare, walking ahead, "Get out of my way before a tiny elephant crushes a big hare like you!"